THE ADVENTURES OF Captain Pugwash

The Boat Race

RED FOX

A Red Fox Book

Published by Random House Children's Books
20 Vauxhall Bridge Road, London SW1V 2SA

A division of The Random House Group Ltd
London Melbourne Sydney Auckland
Johannesburg and agencies throughout the world

The Adventures of Captain Pugwash
Created by John Ryan
© Britt Allcroft (Development) Limited 2000
All rights worldwide Britt Allcroft (Development) Limited
CAPTAIN PUGWASH is a trademark of Britt Allcroft (Development) Limited
THE BRITT ALLCROFT COMPANY is a trademark of The Britt Allcroft Company plc

Cover illustration by Ian Hillyard
Inside illustrations by Red Central Limited

Text adapted by Sally Byford from the original TV story

1 3 5 7 9 10 8 6 4 2

THE RANDOM HOUSE GROUP Limited Reg. No. 954009

www.randomhouse.co.uk

ISBN 0 09 940818 X

Captain Pugwash was very excited. The Governor of
Portobello was holding a boat race and the prize was
one hundred gold doubloons.

"Tottering turtles!" cried Pugwash. "We've got to win!"

But Pugwash's old enemy, Cut-throat Jake, had also entered
the race, and he was determined to win, too.

In his mansion, the Governor explained the rules. "Now, gentlemen," he said. "The race will start at Compass Point. When I fire the cannon, you must sail all the way around Cutlass Island. When the first ship passes the finishing flag here," – he pointed at the map – "I'll fire the cannon again. And may the best man win!"

When the Governor had gone, Cut-throat Jake moved closer to Pugwash. "Let's make a bet," he said. "If you win, you take my ship, the Flying Dustman, if I win, I take the Black Pig.'

Pugwash wasn't happy, but he didn't want to look like a coward. "I - well - er - yes, I'll accept your bet, Jake," he said, "and look forward to winning fair and square."

"Who said anything about being fair?" snarled Jake.

Pugwash hurried back to his ship and made the crew start practising their sailing skills.

"Jake's crew aren't doing any practice," grumbled Jonah.

"Well, they'll be sorry," said Pugwash. "Now, let's try hauling the anchor and hoisting the sails." But the crew couldn't do anything right, so Pugwash gave up and went for lunch.

Tom was worried. He didn't
think the Black Pig could
win. While Pugwash ate his
lunch, Tom studied the map.
"We'll have to watch out for
these mud flats, Captain,
they could be a problem,"
he said, pointing to the map.
"Or perhaps we should just
pull out of the race. Then
Jake can't possibly take our ship."

"Stuttering starfish, Tom," cried Pugwash
crossly. "I'm not listening to that
kind of talk. Go to your cabin
and stay there. We'll win
without you."

The night before the race, Tom heard noises on deck and he crept out of his cabin to investigate. Cut-throat Jake and his crew had crept aboard the Black Pig and were cutting through the ropes of the ship's wheel.

"Now Pugwash won't stand a chance tomorrow," hissed Jake.

Tom knew it was up to him to save the Black Pig. He'd soon
thought of a clever plan and collected together a cannon and
a flag.

No one saw Tom as he rowed out towards Cutlass Island.

In the morning, the Governor arrived at Compass Point to start the race. Cut-throat Jake was ready for action, but Pugwash and his crew had just woken up.

"Where's Tom?" they wailed. "Where's our breakfast?"

"On your marks… Get set…" shouted the Governor.
"We're not quite ready," stuttered Pugwash,
stumbling on deck in his nightshirt.
"Go!" The Governor fired the cannon.

The Flying Dustman sailed off at once. "I'll be waiting for you at the finishing line, Pugwash," bellowed Jake. "You can hand over your ship then!'

"You haven't won yet," cried Pugwash, as his crew scrambled about the deck.

At last they got the Black Pig moving, but it wasn't sailing in a straight line.

"Captain!" called Jonah, "We're heading for the mud flats."

"Shivering sharks. Do something!" Pugwash shouted to Willy, who was trying to steer.

"There's something funny about this wheel," said Willy.

There was nothing they could do.
The Black Pig floated onto the
mud flats, where it stuck fast.
"Doddering dolphins," wailed
Pugwash. "We've lost the race,
and Jake will get the Black Pig."

While Pugwash's crew tried to push their ship out of the mud, the Flying Dustman sailed easily round Cutlass Island, and passed the finishing flag.

The cannon fired and Jake roared, "We've won!"

Dook, Swine and Stinka cheered.

"I can't wait to see Pugwash's face when he hands the Black Pig over to me!" chuckled Jake.

Jake and his crew were soon celebrating their win. They hadn't seen Tom hiding on Cutlass Island with a cannon and flag.

"I've just one more job to do," said Tom, "and then I'll go back to the Black Pig. I expect the Captain will be needing my help."

The Black Pig was
still stuck when
Tom returned.
  "Where have you
been?" cried Pugwash.
"Jake has won. We
heard the cannon."

"That wasn't the finishing
gun," said Tom. "That was me!
Don't worry, Captain, Jake
hasn't won yet. The tide is
coming in now, so we'll
soon float off the mud flats.
We can still win the race."

Tom quickly mended the wheel. When the tide came in, the Black Pig was ready to go. They sailed around Cutlass Island and past the Flying Dustman, where Jake and his crew were dozing on the deck.

"Hey, boss," cried Dook. "There's the Black Pig."

Jake leapt to his feet. "You've lost, Pugwash!" he roared. "We finished hours ago."

When the Black Pig sailed past the finishing flag, the crowd cheered as the Governor fired his cannon for the real winners. Behind them, Jake was shaking his fists. "But we won!" he shouted. He didn't realise that the Flying Dustman was slowly drifting onto some rocks.

There was a loud crash. The Flying Dustman hit the rocks and
Jake and his crew were thrown to the floor

On the Black Pig, the Governor presented Pugwash with a fine trophy and one hundred gold doubloons. "Congratulations," he said. "You did very well."

Just then a soaking-wet Jake clambered aboard. "Give me that," he growled. "I won."

"Oh no," said the Governor. "You stopped half a mile short."

"Don't worry, Jake," said Pugwash. "I won't hold you to your bet. I don't want your ship now that it's such a wreck!"

Jake roared with anger and fell into the sea with a splash.

Tom smiled as he made tea for Pugwash and the Governor.
He was very pleased that the Captain had won the race and the
Black Pig had been saved. Of course, he'd tricked Cut-throat
Jake by moving the finishing flag half a mile away from its
real place. But no one would ever know, would they?